Gar
TITCH

Pat Hutchins

RED FOX

A Red Fox Book

Published by Random House Children's Books
20 Vauxhall Bridge Road, London SW1V 2SA

A division of Random House UK Ltd
London Melbourne Sydney Auckland
Johannesburg and agencies throughout the world

Copyright © Pat Hutchins 1999
Copyright © photographs Hutchins Film Company Limited

A Hutchins Film Company Limited production for Yorkshire Television

1 3 5 7 9 10 8 6 4 2

First published by Red Fox 1999

Printed and bound in Hong Kong.

RANDOM HOUSE UK Limited Reg. No. 954009

ISBN 0 09 940032 4

Titch rode his tricycle into the kitchen.

He and Tailcat had been playing outside, and Mother had just washed the kitchen floor.

'Oh dear!' said Mother, 'just look at that muddy floor! I'll have to wash it again!'

'I'll wash it for you,' said Titch.
'Then I'm going to help Peter
and Mary in the garden.'

Peter was busy watering the garden when Titch cycled out.

Titch stopped his bike.
'Can I help you water the
garden, Peter?' he asked.

'You can't,' said Peter. 'The water's stopped coming out of the hosepipe.'

Titch didn't realise what was stopping it.

'It's funny,' said Peter, 'it was working before you came out.'

'I'll go and help Mary then,' said Titch, and he pedalled his tricycle towards Mary.

The water came out again. *swoosh!*

'Titch!' shouted Peter. 'I'm soaking!'

No wonder the water wasn't coming out of the hosepipe – the wheel of Titch's tricycle was squashing it down!

Titch cycled towards Mary.

'I don't want your help until I come back,' said Mary. 'I know what you're like! You might do something wrong.'

But Titch couldn't wait for Mary to come back.
He wanted to surprise her.

'I'll put these plants in for her,' he told Tailcat. 'She'll be very pleased.'

Mary wasn't pleased. 'Titch!' she cried. 'You've just planted all the weeds I pulled up. Why don't you go away and do something else!'

So Titch and Tailcat looked for something else to do.
  'Look at all those weeds, Tailcat,' said Titch. 'I'll
pull them up.'

But they weren't weeds.
They were Dad's prize spinach.
'Just look what you've done, Titch!' cried Peter and Mary.

'Dad will be very cross with you… and here he comes!'

But Dad wasn't cross. He wasn't cross at all.
'Well done, Titch,' he said. 'I was coming to pick the spinach for supper, and you've done it for me!'

So Titch carried the spinach into the kitchen.

'Come on, Tailcat,' said Titch, 'this spinach needs washing. It's very muddy.'